Hi! I'm Eddie.
Eddie Carlson.

This is a story about me
and my three best friends
– Haggis, Fiend and Norman.
They're monsters.

They're big **Monsters**. Big hairy

...ement of
the h.... Don't tell anyone, will you?
They're a secret. Only me, my parents
and my big sister Angela
know about them.
And it isn't easy keeping
it that way . . .

Eddie

*With special thanks to
Ian Pike*

For more monster mess and chaos,
try reading:
Me & My Monsters: Monsters in the Basement!
Me & My Monsters: Monster School!
Me & My Monsters: Monster Mess!

Based on a script entitled
Call of The Mild by Mark Huckerby
and Nick Ostler

Me and My Monsters is co-created by
Mark Grant and Claudia Lloyd

Me & My
MONSTERS™

Monster
Manners

RORY GROWLER

PUFFIN

PUFFIN BOOKS

Published by the Penguin Group
Penguin Books Ltd, 80 Strand, London WC2R 0RL, England
Penguin Group (USA) Inc., 375 Hudson Street, New York, New York 10014, USA
Penguin Group (Canada), 90 Eglinton Avenue East,
Suite 700, Toronto, Ontario, Canada M4P 2Y3
(a division of Pearson Penguin Canada Inc.)
Penguin Ireland, 25 St Stephen's Green, Dublin 2, Ireland
(a division of Penguin Books Ltd)
Penguin Group (Australia), 250 Camberwell Road, Camberwell, Victoria 3124, Australia
(a division of Pearson Australia Group Pty Ltd)
Penguin Books India Pvt Ltd, 11 Community Centre,
Panchsheel Park, New Delhi – 110 017, India
Penguin Group (NZ), 67 Apollo Drive, Rosedale, Auckland 0632, New Zealand
(a division of Pearson New Zealand Ltd)
Penguin Books (South Africa) (Pty) Ltd, 24 Sturdee Avenue,
Rosebank, Johannesburg 2196, South Africa

Penguin Books Ltd, Registered Offices: 80 Strand, London WC2R 0RL, England

puffinbooks.com

First published 2011
001 – 10 9 8 7 6 5 4 3 2 1

Copyright © Tiger Aspect Productions/The Jim Henson Company/Sticky Pictures Pty Ltd 2011
Me & My Monsters ™ & © Tiger Aspect Productions/The Jim Henson Company/
Sticky Pictures Pty Ltd 2011
Me & My Monsters is produced by Tiger Aspect Productions, The Jim Henson Company
and Sticky Pictures Pty Ltd
All rights reserved

Set in Futura Standard
Printed in Great Britain by Clays Ltd, St Ives plc

British Library Cataloguing in Publication Data
A CIP catalogue record for this book is available from the British Library

ISBN: 978-0-141-33670-1

www.greenpenguin.co.uk

MIX
Paper from
responsible sources
FSC™ C018179

Penguin Books is committed to a sustainable
future for our business, our readers and our
planet. This book is made from paper certified
by the Forest Stewardship Council.

Spiders! Eek!

'Bzzzzzzzttt!'

'Interesting,' said Dad.

I was sitting at the kitchen table watching Dad trying to change the light bulb in a lamp. But every time Dad looked away, Norman would pick up the old light bulb with his teeth and make a funny buzzing noise. Then all the lights in the house would go out, and the bulb in his mouth would glow brightly.

'Nnngggsssttttt.'

The bulb in Norman's mouth lit up again. I grinned as his fur stood on end, making him look like a big purple fluffball. *What a skill*, I thought.

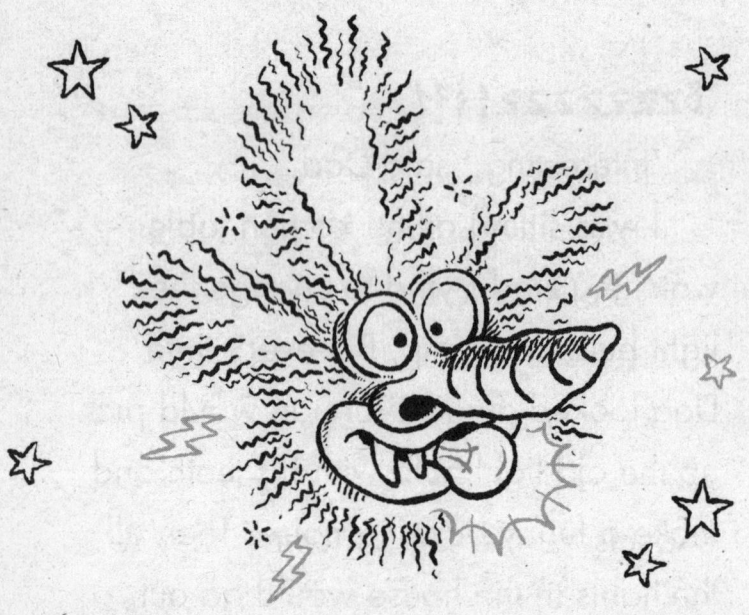

I often thought that when I watched my monsters do something amazing.

'Yes, all right, very clever,' said

Dad. 'Now will you please get him out of here?' Dad was starting to get cross with the lamp, I could tell. He always did when he was trying to fix something and it wouldn't work.

You must have noticed how, when you're a kid, grown-ups are always bossing you about. They're always telling you to change. Change that face you're pulling, change your attitude, change your underwear more than once a week. It never stops. *Lucky monsters*, I thought. *No one ever expects them to be something they're not.*

I looked over at Fiend and Haggis, who were 'helping' Mum to fix the pipes under the sink.

7

'Can you pass me a screwdriver?' called Mum, holding out her hand from somewhere under the sink.

'We need a screwdriver!' said Fiend. He was taking charge as usual and ordering Haggis about.

Haggis nodded and found the screwdriver. Well, actually, he picked up the screwdriver in his mouth and chewed it a bit, then let out a big, furry, monster-like **'Buuurp!'**

'Will *someone* please hand me a

8

screwdriver?' Mum's legs were starting to twitch under the sink. A sure sign she was getting fed up.

'**Boop, weedle.**' Norman reached in and fished out the screwdriver from Haggis's mouth. It was now covered in sticky monster drool, the kind you could glue bricks together with.

'**Eeeewwww...yuuuuck!**' said Mum as Norman handed it over. 'This is so *not* how I had planned on spending the day. I don't know why the plumbing has been playing up so much recently.' She gave up and crawled out from under the sink to dry off. She had been under there for some time with

9

a spanner. Looking at the state of her, there had been a lot of dirty water leaking out of those pipes.

'Do you want me to take a look under the sink?' offered Dad. 'I'm quite the expert when it comes to DIY.' He was flicking the lamp switch on and off, confused as to why the new bulb wasn't lighting up.

'How many Carlsons does it take to change a light bulb?' grinned Mum.

'Bing!' Norman answered, but Dad just sighed. He could tell the joke was at his expense.

'One,' Mum smiled smugly. 'Just not *you*, darling.' She held up the lead to the lamp, showing him that the reason the lamp wasn't working was because it wasn't plugged in. Dad grabbed the plug off her as if to say 'I knew that', just as Fiend began emptying everything in the toolbox on to the floor.

'Hey!' cried Mum. 'Hands out of there! Don't mess with my system. I have a *place* for everything and *everything* in its place.'

'Speaking of which,' said Dad, standing up crossly, 'isn't it time for certain furry freeloaders to go back down to their basement?'

'Oh, can't we stay up here just a little bit longer, human mum lady?' Fiend pleaded. 'It's not like we're doing any *harm*.'

Just then, a loud groaning noise started coming from the sink. It was like the sound of pressure building up. Mum and Dad looked at each other with puzzled faces. The groaning noise started to get louder and louder, and then suddenly both taps flew out from the sink and shot around the room like fighter jets looking to land in enemy territory. A second later there was a loud **CRASH!** and the sound of breaking glass.

There was a stunned silence as everyone watched Norman crawl out from under the sink.

'What?' said Fiend, looking around at everyone. 'It's not supposed to do that?'

I shut my eyes as Mum and Dad
pointed towards the door.

'Basement!' they yelled.

'NOW!'

Life Sucks

'It's unbelievable!' I said, pacing around the monsters' basement den.

'Unbelievable,' agreed Haggis, trailing after me.

'In fact, it stinks!'

'Yeah, it stinks!' Haggis looked at me, confused. 'What are we angry about again, Eddie?'

'You guys getting banished from upstairs again!' I flopped down on to the monsters' sofa.

'And we were being so *helpful*, too,' added Fiend.

'Yeah, we're always helpful,' agreed Haggis. 'Just the other night

we found a new spider the size of a football and we made him a *special* new home.'

I had big problems on my mind, but wow, a spider the size of a football? I'd never seen that before.

'The size of a football?' I said.

'Seriously?'

'Yeah! Look!' Haggis pointed at a big mess of pipes in a corner of the basement.

I moved in for a closer look. The monsters had bent and knotted the pipes together to make a home for the spider. I could see some giant furry legs poking out from between the pipes and cobwebs.

'Whoa, he's a beast!'

'We even came up with a special name for him,' said Haggis proudly. 'Eddie, meet . . . Large Spider!'

'That's very . . . accurate,' I grinned.

'It was a long three days coming up with that name, I can tell you!' said Fiend proudly.

I leaned over to take a closer look at the knotted and bent pipes. You could hear water rushing and gurgling about inside them. They looked like pretty important pipes to me; the kind that lead to the boiler and water supply, if you know the sort I mean. The kind of pipes you really didn't want to mess with.

'Hang on,' I said slowly, as an idea formed in my head. 'Are you telling me that *you* did this to the water pipes? To make a home

for Large Spider?'

Fiend smiled proudly, nodding his head. 'It's all our own handiwork. It's *impressive*, huh?'

'That explains the plumbing problems upstairs! You've twisted all those pipes into a ball and ruined the whole water system!'

Haggis puffed out his chest, taking it all as one enormous compliment. I tried to reason with them. 'Listen, if the pipes burst you won't be able to live down here . . .' I stopped short,

realizing what I had just said. The monsters were all gazing at me with puzzled faces.

'Just think,' I said, trying to explain to them. 'The smallest knock might make these pipes spring a leak and flood the basement. Then you'll *have* to stay upstairs!'

I hesitated, knowing what I was about to do would be very, very wrong, but still worth it. I held out my hand to Fiend.

'Pass me the screwdriver.' I jammed it into the knot of pipes. We all waited for a second. Nothing happened. Then a second longer. Still nothing. Then

21

a few more moments. Then something did happen. Something very, very big and a bit like a tidal wave.

One Big Splash

We gathered in the hallway to dry off.

'Well, that worked slightly better than expected,' I said as Haggis shook himself dry like an oversized puppy that had just had a bath. Dad came in looking cross.

'Come on, Eddie, didn't you hear me calling? It's time for dinner.' He frowned as he spotted the monsters.

'Hey, I thought we agreed. They were going to stay downstairs in the basement or I call pest control. And why is there water everywhere?'

'Er, we'd love to go back to the basement Mr C,' began Fiend. 'But the, er, *damp* problem seems to have got a teensy, tiny bit *worse*.' Fiend was now using the end of one of the curtains to dry himself off. Dad just laughed at him.

'The damp? Since when do monsters worry about damp?' And with that, he set off down to the basement to see for himself. I did try to warn him about the water. I could be helpful like that – sometimes.

'Er, Dad. You might want to wait . . .'

But it was too late.

SPLASH!

A second later he came back, looking very embarrassed and like he had jumped into a very deep swimming pool.

'I think I might just grab a towel,' he muttered. To be fair, he was taking all of this a lot better than I had expected. A while later (and after Dad had got changed), we were all called into the kitchen for a family meeting. Usually, this meant I was in trouble for not keeping the monsters in line or that Haggis had left a really bad smell somewhere. But this time it was different. Mum cleared her throat and began the meeting.

'Right, here's the deal. The

basement is officially flooded so the monsters will have to stay upstairs for dinner.'

'Yes!' I shouted, punching the air with my fist. Mum gave me a look.

'I mean, er, yeah, I suppose that's true.' I shrugged, trying to play down my excitement in case she got suspicious.

Mum carried on. 'And they'll have to stay upstairs while your father very sweetly tries to prove to me that he's not completely useless at fixing stuff.'

'**Woo-hoo!**' cheered Norman.

I looked at Dad. He was dressed

in waterproof trousers, clutching his toolbox. He waved his wrench in the air.

'Some say DIY,' he declared. 'I say D-I-*WHY*-not!' I don't know exactly what he meant by that, but it seemed to make him feel brave. And then he was on his way back to the basement, this time, hopefully, more prepared for what was down there.

'Thanks, Mum,' I grinned. 'You

won't regret this.' I really was pleased.
The monsters were staying for tea; it
didn't get any better than that.

'I just hope you guys can show
me that you know how to behave
like grown-ups.' Mum smiled at them
sweetly.

The first part of the plan was
complete, getting the monsters to
stay upstairs. But persuading them to
behave like grown-ups? Even *I* didn't
know how to do that.

Yummy!

We were eating tea. At least we were trying to eat tea. The non-furry members of the Carlson family were not so much eating as trying to dodge food. The furry ones were just kind of chasing it about and throwing stuff.

'Stay still, wriggly worm!' shouted Haggis, trying to grab a piece of spaghetti.

'Gweeb,' called out Norman as he threw some grated cheese into the air and tried to catch it on his nose.

'Isn't this nice?' said Mum, sounding a bit desperate. 'All of us humans and monsters having dinner together for the first and, without a doubt, last time.'

I couldn't answer: I was busy watching Fiend. He'd been sniffing the pepper pot and had now started twitching, and rocking back and forth. These were all warning signs that some sort of monster explosion was about to happen.

'Ah, ah, ah . . .' Fiend started.

'Eddie, what's happening?' said Mum, sounding worried.

Angela noticed it next. She nodded at me: it was time to take cover.

'Ahhh . . . Ahhh . . .

. . . ACHHHOOOO!'

Ewwww. Fiend's monster sneeze
had covered half the table in yucky,
green, Fiend-style gunk.

'Now that's what I call *seasoning*,'
he grinned.

'Fiend!' I cried. I couldn't believe
it. This was our one shot at getting the
monsters to stay upstairs and he was –
quite literally – blowing it!

'Excuse me, Mum,' I said and
moved down the table to where Fiend
was sitting, to try to get him to behave.
It didn't work. Every time I waved my
finger at him, he tried to bite it.

Mum was looking around the table
with a sort of quiet shock. Angela
could sense Mum's guard was down.
That sort of thing doesn't happen very

often round here, so you really have to seize your moment when it does.

'So, Mum,' she started. 'It's really cool how laid-back you are. You're the kind of parent who doesn't say no. You're the sort that lets us *experience* new things, and that's why you're so great.' I rolled my eyes. Sisters have no skill when it comes to fooling a mother.

Mum gave Angela a look. She

wasn't falling for it. Funny how she never seems to. I guess it's the same in your house.

'Out with it, Angela,' grinned Mum. 'You must want something, so what is it?'

Angela hesitated then took a deep breath. 'Everyone's going to this movie tomorrow night, and I really want to go as well. But strictly speaking, it's sort of for over-fifteens only.'

Angela tried her best *oooh-look-at-me-I'm-really-sweet-and-innocent* face, but Mum was having none of it. Sisters are amateurs, see? They never learn.

'What kind of film?' asked Mum.

'Ah, well,' bluffed Angela. 'I guess you could call it a romantic comedy

with a hint of adventure.'

'Title?' You had to give Mum credit; she was good with the questions.

Angela stared at the floor. *Undead Zombie Freaks Wreck Britain,*' she mumbled.

'NO!' cried Mum. 'Not in a million years!'

'But you don't even know what it's about yet!' argued Angela.

Mum was about to explain that the title of the film kind of said it all, when suddenly there was a huge

Haggis had jumped on to the table,
crushing everything under him in true
Haggis style.

'GOT YOU, WRIGGLY
WORM!'

he cried, holding up a piece of spaghetti.
Poor Haggis. He'd destroyed most of
the table, but he'd not given up trying
to eat his grown-up dinner.

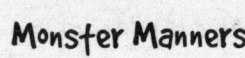

I looked around the floor at all of
the broken plates. Then I tried that
'being positive' thing Mum had
been doing earlier.

'Er, think of all
the washing-up this is
saving you?'

'*Eddie . . .*' Mum muttered, starting
to lose her cool. It was time for me to
admit defeat.

'All right, all right,'
I said. 'I'll take the
monsters back to
the basement.'

'No can do, sorry!'
shouted Dad, staggering
back into the kitchen. He looked worn
out from his DIY adventures.

'Why can't they go back downstairs?' sighed Mum.

'Well, it's like this,' said Dad, flopping into a chair. 'I was down there in the basement trying to mend the pipes, but then suddenly I had to defend myself against this mega spider . . .'

'Darn it,' muttered Fiend, slapping himself on the head. 'That's a much better name.'

'And the thing is,' Dad went on, 'it seems that, in bravely defending myself from Mega Spider, I may have made the leak a tiny bit bigger. So it's going to be at least twenty-four hours till the place is habitable again. Which means a day off work for me tomorrow. DIY-ing it, baby.'

He was now helping himself to a piece of chicken in the hope that his speech somehow made up for everything, but he was really fooling no one.

Mum sighed deeply. You know, the way mums do.

'OK, OK. Eddie, make up some beds. The monsters can sleep in your room tonight.'

'**Gribble, dank, chuppa!**' Norman cheered excitedly. 'Norman says *Yay!*' explained Fiend. And I knew exactly what he meant.

Sweet Dreams

'Right,' said Mum.
'NO midnight
feasts, NO
pillow fights and
NO jumping on
the bed.' She
was keen to lay down a few ground
rules when it came to a sleepover.

Fiend looked disappointed. I knew
what he was thinking. He'd been
planning on bouncing high enough on
the bed to shoot through the ceiling
and up into the attic. He'd done it once
or twice before, and must have been

keen for another go. Unfortunately, Mum hadn't forgotten.

'Do I make myself clear?' she said, looking directly at Fiend.

'**Bing boop,**' Norman answered for everyone.

'Crystal,' I said quickly.

Mum gave us her best *don't-make-me-come-back-in-again* look and then turned the light off and headed out of the room.

I counted three seconds before I had to turn the light back on. You wouldn't think three monsters could make such a mess in such a short space of time.

Norman put down his pillow sheepishly, Haggis tried to hide a bag

of crisps behind his back and Fiend
stopped jumping up and down on
the bed.

'Come on, guys!' I said. 'Not
tonight, OK? This is your shot at going
totally free-range. You can't afford to
blow it now.'

'Sorry, Ed,' said Fiend. 'But this
whole "being sensible" gig, it doesn't
come naturally to us.

'WE'RE BORN TO MISBEHAVE!'

'Tough,' I argued. 'I mean it. You've
got to change. In fact, right now I'm
enrolling you in Eddie's Night School.
And the first topic is *How
to Act Grown-up.*

Some might say I was being harsh,
but it was for their own good. If they
didn't change, they'd be sent back to
the basement forever. This was their
big chance to stay upstairs and I had
to make the most of it!

Lesson one was *How to Brush
Your Teeth*. I have to say, the monsters
scored ten out of ten for enthusiasm.
It was just a shame that none of
them actually used a real toothbrush.
Fiend tried cleaning his teeth with my
hairbrush, and Haggis attempted to
clean his teeth with the toilet brush.
To be fair, at least the toilet brush
was the right size for Haggis's mouth,
so I couldn't really argue. Norman
did use an actual toothbrush, but he

decided that as he didn't like the taste of toothpaste, he would use ice cream instead. I'm not a dentist, but I'm fairly sure that defeats the point.

The next lesson was called *Using a Knife and Fork*. Again, Norman got points for being the only monster to actually use a knife or a fork, but I'm fairly sure it will take Dad a long time to get that fork out of the wall once he finds it. Still, Norman did better than Haggis who thought his knife and fork looked a bit small, and decided to try using a garden rake and a cricket bat instead. Norman also definitely did better than Fiend. Fiend was willing to use a fork, but not prepared to hold it with his hands, so he lost lots of points for disgusting table manners.

The final lesson was called *How to Use the Toilet* and the less said on this tricky subject the better. So overall, there was still a lot of work to do.

However, some of the lessons must have made a difference, because there was a definite change in the monsters' behaviour as became clear over the next day or so.

More Tea, Vicar?

'We're terribly, quite amazingly sorry about breaking the table, human woman mum,' said Fiend. 'It was terribly **MONSTERISH** of us.'

I stared at Fiend. This wasn't like him at all. Oh, well, perhaps he was planning something Fiendish.

'Er, apology accepted. Thanks, Fiend,' said Mum, also puzzled at Fiend's new manners. We were all back in the kitchen, having another go at eating together. This time it was lunch.

'Please, would you like more tea, please, Mrs Carlson?' Haggis was doing it, too, trying to be polite.

'Er, thanks, Haggis,' said Mum.

'No, thank YOU.' Haggis actually curtseyed this time.

Just then Norman leaned forward and breathed heavily over her.

'Whoa! Not so close, Norman.' She hesitated for a second and then sniffed Norman a little more closely. Not something I would ever have done, but I guess mums have to do some pretty unpleasant stuff when they're in charge of kids and monsters. Like checking whether your teeth are clean or you've washed behind your ears.

'Actually, that's minty-fresh breath, Norm.' Mum was impressed. Norman smiled proudly.

'**wheek, grubdle, glotch.**' Then he bowed. Mum looked just as shocked as I was.

'Did he just say thank you?'

'He did,' said Fiend, stepping forward to help. 'And *I* have also successfully used the toilet this morning, and I only fell in ONCE!'

Right, now I was starting to get really suspicious. Why on earth was Fiend talking like he was having a conversation with the Queen?

I didn't really have much time to get to the bottom of it as Angela had wandered into the kitchen looking

cross. She had the Angry Sister look. 'Monsters living in the basement I can just about deal with,' she started. 'But monsters using my shower and using my loofah? **NOT HAPPY!**'

She brought out her loofah, a sticky, woolly, big sponge thing that was now covered in red monster fur. She waved it at Haggis, who couldn't really deny being responsible given the colour of the fur.

'Well, I for one am impressed our monsters are really changing their ways!' said Mum. 'I thought you'd be pleased, Angela.'

Angela wasn't pleased. 'I just don't see why Eddie's allowed to have his friends around twenty-four seven, but I'm not allowed to see one zombie apocalypse movie.'

'Look, sweetie,' said Mum. 'I've checked out the other films at the cinema – how about *High School Hoedown*? Square-dancing isn't just for squares, you know. I'll even come with you! How about it?'

Angela was horrified and I can't say I blamed her. I mean, there was *no way* I would go to see a film about dancing, with my mother. Angela shook her head in despair.

'I am just going to walk away with what little remains of my dignity,' she sighed.

With that, she turned towards the door, her head held high. Well, for a brief second anyway. Norman and Fiend had been helping Mum mop the floor earlier and it was still really wet. Angela slipped, her legs flying up in the air, and landed flat on her bottom.

I sniggered and waited for the monsters
to start laughing at her really, really
loudly, but nothing happened. It was all
quite worrying.

Then Fiend leaned over to my mum,
like they were in a library, and said
quietly, 'I very much want to laugh my
head off right now, but I guess that
wouldn't be very grown-up, would it?'
Mum nodded at him as if to say, 'Wise
words, Fiend. Wise words.'

Right, now I was *really* suspicious.

Who Stole My Monsters?

The next day I got home from school and burst into the living room to see the monsters.

'Hey, you guys, Mum and Dad are out so we are free to P-A-R-T-Y!'

But instead of the usual monster madness I expected to find, I saw Fiend sitting on the sofa, reading the newspaper and listening to classical music. Well, he was doing his best to pretend that he was reading it.

I could hear Haggis and Norman in
the kitchen doing some sort of chore or
other. I know. It was all very weird.
I decided to try to liven things up a bit.

I changed the radio station and
started dancing. Then I stopped.
Fiend had turned the radio off
and was looking at me with
one eyebrow raised.

'What's up, Fiend?' I said. He
normally loved dancing round the living
room when Mum and Dad were out.

'What's up?' said Fiend. 'Hmmnnn
. . . The ceiling and the light bulb are
what's up. And as for what's down –
I think we both know that jacket does
NOT belong on the floor, young man.
Hm, does it? No, it does not!'

I stared at Fiend and decided I was wasting my time. Instead, I headed into the kitchen.

'Help me, Norm. What's old grouchy knickers Fiend in a mood about?'

'Binglo, scratchum.' Now I had no idea what Norman had said, but right now I actually didn't care. I had spotted something else worrying.

'Bay leaves, cloves . . . Norm! Have you alphabetized the spice rack?'

'Jipling, sweetchy coot!' he replied. Another lost cause. I suddenly realized what was going on.

'Oh, I get it!' I said. 'You're still acting grown-up, aren't you? It's OK, Mum and Dad aren't here. You can drop the act. Tell them, Haggis.'

'*Hello, Edward!*' said Haggis, turning round from the sink to greet me. He'd been doing the washing-up. He was waving a dishcloth and wearing an apron. It was all too much for me.

'OK,' I managed to say. 'Now I'm totally freaked out.'

Fiend appeared in the kitchen. 'In that case, Eddie,' he said. 'Why don't you just sit down nicely and tell us how your day at school was? Hm? Please, thank you, may I? Hmnn?'

They had all gone crazy, and not in a good way.

'Guys! Snap out of it!' I cried out in despair.

'Snap out of what, honey?' Haggis said as he started dusting. Dusting I tell you!

'All this grown-up stuff. It's just not you.' Then I had a brainwave. Something drastic was called for so I decided to pull out all the stops.

'I know, let's play . . . *Name That Trumpy Armpit Tune*. I'll go first.'

I knew this was a sure-fire way to get them to see sense so I stuffed my hand under my armpit and began pumping away to make the loudest sounds possible.

'**Zonk.**' Norman was staring at me like I had trodden in something.

'You're right, Norman, that is
disgusting,' said Fiend. Haggis was a
bit more smiley, but even he couldn't be
relied on, because he was now busy
chopping parsley.

'Dinner's in twenty minutes, dear
boy,' he told me.

Then it hit me. It was a lot worse
than I thought. I came right out with
it. Well, you have to be direct when
things get this serious.

'I know what's wrong,' I said.
'You've been upstairs for too long,
guys. You've been brainwashed.
You've . . . you've . . .' I could barely
bring myself to say it . . .

'YOU'VE GROWN UP!'

Time to Go Home

I sat in the corner, sulking. I'd tried to explain to my family what had happened to the monsters and get them to help me fix it. But they weren't listening as usual.

Instead, Angela was *still* trying to convince Mum to let her go and see the new zombie film. Now she was pretending to read out a review from the newspaper.

'I quote . . .' she said, clearing her throat. 'The film is a masterpiece.'

'Who said that?' asked Mum suspiciously, peering at the paper. 'A newspaper critic?'

'Er, no,' confessed Angela. 'Just one of my friends, but they really know what they're talking about.'

'The answer is *no*, Angela. You can't go and see the film.' Like I said before, you have to get up pretty early to fool Mum.

'**N–O,**' joined in Fiend.

'Please, Mum,' begged Angela.

'Everyone is going.'

'No, they're not,' argued Mum.

'They're not you know, little lady!' echoed Fiend. He had clearly decided to take Mum's side. Nothing would surprise me right now, even two old enemies closing ranks.

'This family is insane!' shouted Angela, storming off.

'Did you see how I improvized there?' said Fiend to Mum. 'That little-lady thing just sort of came to me. Wow! I'm really getting the hang of this *grown-up* stuff. If anyone asks you a question, you just say **NO**! It's fun!'

Mum looked at him oddly. I guess he had pushed it one step too far.

'Maybe you should let me deal with

the kids, OK, Fiend?' she said. 'Now look, the news is on TV and I want to watch it.'

Fiend leapt up excitedly. 'Is it that the time already?' he asked. 'I'm dying to see how that whole *fishing quota* story has developed in the last half-hour.' I rolled my eyes and buried my head in a cushion. Fiend was just settling down in front of the telly when Dad came back in, wearing overalls and clutching his spanner. 'Great news, guys, the basement is all dried out.'

As one, the monsters stopped what they were doing and looked at him. Then they looked at Mum.

'Did you hear that? You can go home!' She obviously thought they would be pleased.

Finally, Fiend piped up, keeping one eye on the news as he did so.

'Gosh, Kate, that's a *jolly kind* offer. It really is, but we rather think we might *prefer* to stay *upstairs*.' The other two nodded as Mum and Dad began panicking.

'What are you saying exactly?' squeaked Dad.

Fiend looked thoughtful. 'I suppose we're saying . . . *thanks* . . . but *no thanks*.'

And with that, he went back to watching the news, as casual as can be.

Enough Is Enough
Is Enough!

We were back in the monsters'
basement den. The monsters had
refused to go back down to the
basement so we had escaped there
ourselves for a secret family meeting.
I was watching Mum and Dad pace
around the floor.

You had to feel sorry for them.
Having the monsters permanently
upstairs was a bit like getting nits.
Once they'd bedded in, they were
almost impossible to shift.

'They just hang around all day
long, getting under our feet, interfering

with our stuff, asking us for more tea,' cried Mum.

'It's just like having your grandmother to stay, but with more hair,' muttered Dad.

'The trouble is they're just so polite when they tell us how happy they are,'

72

Mum carried on. 'It's almost impossible to come up with a reason to get rid of them. It's enough to drive me mad.'

'It's not natural,' agreed Dad. 'Monsters are meant to be a pain. I tell you, I'm not sure how much more of this I can handle.'

I looked at them both, sharing their grief. We were all united in a common cause. We wanted our monsters back and I had an idea about how to do it. I rallied the troops.

'I think I might know what to do,' I said.

They stared at me. To be honest, they were looking so desperate I think they would have tried anything.

'Fiend, Haggis and Norman turned this way just from watching how you behave, right?'

Mum and Dad nodded.

'OK, in that case I have a plan. But you have to do exactly what I tell you. And I warn you, it could get messy.'

I waved them in close and began to whisper. It was a sneaky plan, but I was fairly sure it might just get us out of the mess we were currently in.

That's Disgusting, Mum! Well Done!

We were eating dinner again. Only this time it was a special meal made by Haggis.

'Mmm, that classic combination of uncooked spaghetti, raw onions and . . .' Mum prodded the dish closely in the hope of identifying all the ingredients. She held up something for Angela to see. My sister pulled a face.

'Hey, that's one of my shoes!'

Haggis looked around happily.

'All the ingredients are fresh!' he added.

Fiend leaned back in his chair and raised a glass.

'So, isn't this nice? All of us humans and monsters having a civilized dinner together. Do help yourselves, everyone.'

Mum looked at me. I nodded. It was time to put our plan into action. She took a deep breath, grabbed a lump of food with her hand and gobbled at it in true monster style. I smiled at her to let her know she was doing well.

Angela on the other hand was
completely shocked.

'Mum! You're being a pig.'

I turned to Dad. 'Maybe Angela
would like some dinner?'

He looked nervous, but knew what
had to happen.

'Yeah, yeah, sure, sure thing,'
he said and then scooped a load of
onions out of the bowl
and dropped them
on Angela's
head. She was
too shocked to
say anything.
Dad pushed
home his
advantage.

'Dressing?' And with that, he grabbed a bottle of sauce and smeared it all over her horrified face.

'And you say I'M not grown-up enough?' She couldn't believe it. Neither could the monsters; they were staring at Mum and Dad in disbelief.

'Mr C! what are you playing at?'

Fiend was open-mouthed with shock.

'It's called having fun, *remember*?' Dad now had the shoe out of the dish and was balancing it on his head while

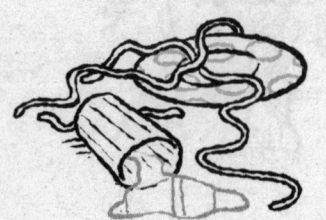 across the table Mum was throwing spaghetti at everyone.

78

'Woo-hoo!
Yeah!' she shouted.
'Look at me, I'm
firing missiles!'

Haggis looked as though he might
faint with horror, but Fiend held up a
hand as if he had the answer to all the
madness before him.

'Wow, all of this has really made
me think.'

Haggis and Norman looked at
Fiend, waiting to hear what he had
to say. 'Do you know what we should
do?' Fiend nodded wisely.

'Join in the food fight like the crazy
monsters you are?' I suggested.

'No,' said Fiend, shaking his head.
'We should make a start on the

washing-up! Somebody has to clean up this mess.'

Sometimes you just cannot rely on a monster to do anything right.

Plan B

Mum and Dad had been down in the basement for a while. I headed down the steps to see them, feeling pretty sorry for myself that the plan hadn't worked.

'OK, well, I guess you can't say we didn't try –' I began.

But instead of the crying I was expecting, Mum was wheeling Dad around on an office chair and both of them were now wearing bin liners.

'Woo-hoo!' shouted Mum, giving Dad a quick spin.

I stared in amazement for a second
or two then managed to splutter, 'OK.
I have many, many questions, but I'm
just going to pick one at random. *What
are you wearing?*'

Mum jumped up on to the chair,
too, and they shot past me and crashed
into the wall, laughing like
crazy as they went.

'Do you like
them?' asked
Mum. 'It was my
idea. Why do
boring laundry
when you can
have disposable
clothes?'

'Weeeeeee!'

They were wearing bin bags. Proper bin bags. Mum was giddy with excitement. This was even more worrying than the monsters living upstairs.

'The monsters can't see you,' I tried. 'You can drop the act.'

'What act, Ed-a-roony? Wahh!' Mum was now doing cartwheels as Dad danced in and out of the way.

'I feel sick in a good way!' he shouted.

How would you feel? My world had been turned upside down. First my monsters were behaving like grown-ups and now my grown-ups were behaving like monsters! Nothing was making sense. I stormed back upstairs to find the only member of the family I could think of who might understand. She's not the first person I would usually rely on, but desperate times called for desperate measures. I went in search of my sister.

I found her in the kitchen and described how our parents were busy going crazy in the basement.

'Where's a responsible grown-up when you need one?' she sighed.

'HERE WE ARE!'

cried Fiend, Haggis and Norman, all popping up completely out of nowhere.

'Whoa, what are you doing?'
I asked them.

'*Spying* on you. It's what grown-ups
do.' Fiend offered his explanation as if
it made perfect sense.

'You don't need to worry about
your parents any more. We can do
anything that they used to do for you.
Try us!' Fiend really did seem to think
he had all the answers. This was bad,
very bad.

'This is a disaster,' I muttered to
Angela.

She looked at me sadly then
suddenly smiled. 'Don't be so sure, Ed.
This could be my chance!'

She pointed at Fiend. 'Right,
Fiend. Because you are the reigning

grown-up in this family . . . I would like to ask permission to go to a scary movie tonight with my friends, please.'

I might have known it – never trust a sister. Still, Fiend wasn't going to fall for something that lame.

'Mmmn. Let me think about it . . . OK, I've thought about it. No.' I was right.

'Are you just saying no because that's what Mum does?' Angela asked.

Fiend looked confused. 'No . . . I mean, er . . . I think . . .'

'So can I not go and just stay here all night?' Angela was tying him in knots. Maybe she was cleverer than I thought. Fiend just sort of spluttered, completely lost, bless him.

'So you're not NOT giving me permission to go tonight then?' she shouted, pushing home her advantage.

'No?' said Fiend.

'**GREAT!** I'll see you later then.' And she was off.

'Have fun!' Fiend actually thought he had done a good thing rather than having been completely taken in. Angela smiled at me just before she headed out of the door.

'You know, Ed, you do have your uses sometimes.'

Time For Bed

As I sat, still reeling from recent events both upstairs and down, Haggis came charging in.

'**OOH OOH OOH OOH**, time to watch the news again.' I couldn't remember seeing him as excited as this for a while. I think the last time might have been when he decided to fill Dad's shoes with jam, which should give you some idea of how much he had changed recently.

'Yay!' shouted Fiend, switching on the telly. I decided enough was enough.

'No! This has gone too far. I might have complained about Mum and Dad from time to time, but there's all different stuff that I need them for. You're not real grown-ups!'

'Is this just a delaying tactic to avoid bedtime?' If he was developing that sixth sense of being able to spot things like that, then Fiend really was turning into a parent. I was shocked and told him so.

'No! And how do you even know about the delaying stuff . . . Oh, never mind.' I realized there were more important things to worry about right now.

'What is it you need? Just say the word, son.' Fiend was now wandering over as if to reassure me that all was well. I had news for him – it wasn't. I decided to test them all fully.

'All right, I need a clean football kit for tomorrow.'

Fiend smiled knowingly. 'You're on laundry duty I believe, Norm.'

'Bop, shweep,' said Norman, holding up a tiny set of clothes that my action man might just have been able to squeeze into if he went on a diet. I couldn't believe it.

'What have you done? Do I really look that small?' They seemed a bit hurt at that, as if I had insulted their hard work, which in a way I guess I had.

'No need to take that tone, young Edward. We simply cleaned it like the clever adult grown-ups we are. So, what else?' Fiend really had no idea. If I turned up to training like that . . . I'd be laughed at more than the time Harry our goalkeeper forgot to put his shorts on during a match. I carried on with my list.

'All right then. Mum always makes me a packed lunch for school.'

'Haggis! You were on catering duty, weren't you?'

He stepped forward proudly. 'Yes.

And you know how you're supposed to feed your children five portions of fruit and veg per day?'

I waited nervously as he fished about in the fridge, before producing my lunch box with a flourish.

'Check this out. I call it my pine-occoli-car-ange-anana!'

I peered at a mess of vegetables and fruit all squished together.

'You'll be the envy of all your friends. Ah, don't worry, Edward, we're in charge now and there's nothing we can't handle.'

Suddenly, a loud banging and crashing sound began echoing around the house. Fiend prodded Haggis in the tummy. 'Do you need a snack?'

'That's not my tummy!' he shouted, looking worried suddenly. 'It must be an earthquake!'

'It's not an earthquake. That's the plumbing out of control again.' I started towards the sink, but Fiend stopped me.

'Nobody panic. Mr Fiend has got it all in hand. Norman, fix the plumbing, please.'

I really was worried. It was twice as loud as before.

'This is serious!' I yelled. 'Please don't make it any worse.' But nobody was listening to me. Norman was already under the sink and I knew it wouldn't be too long before this nightmare became even more of a disaster.

I went to find Mum and Dad. It was time to hope they might snap out of their ridiculous way of behaving once they saw how serious the situation had become.

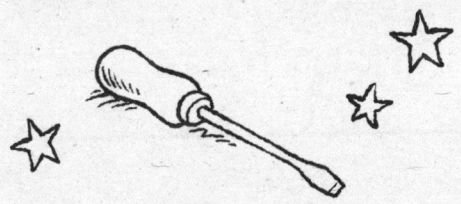

Just When You Thought Things Couldn't Get Any Worse

I didn't have to go too far to find them. They came bouncing in on spacehoppers.

'Woooo! Look at us go! This is awesome!' they shouted, bouncing round and round me like a couple of big kids.

'Mum! Dad! The plumbing's gone crazy! The house is about to explode!' I really was nervous. Luckily, they could sense that drastic action was called for because they stopped bouncing for a second.

'Explosions?' They looked at

each other, concerned, but only for a second.

'Cool! Explosions rock.' And off they bounced again.

I'm afraid to say I lost my temper a bit with them.

'Oh, grow up!' I shouted, rushing back to the kitchen. Well, someone had to take charge before the house blew up. I dashed in to find the monsters still gathered round the sink looking a bit scared all of a sudden.

'It's obvious what's wrong,' Fiend said, poking a tap. 'The pipes must be hungry.'

'Shwish, dribble, glank!' Norman clearly agreed.

'So let's feed them!'

And they were off, with Norman leading the fray, stuffing food under the sink as if his life depended on it. How could they possibly think this might help? Filling a cupboard with food does nothing but produce a bad smell; and we should know because we tried it once when we were really bored during a rainstorm.

'That's it, Norm!' shouted Fiend as a plate of leftover lasagne went in.

'Yes, good! Good work, Haggis!' A bowl of trifle followed.

'That's brilliant, Norman, yes.' The fridge was now nearly totally empty, but that wasn't going to slow them down.

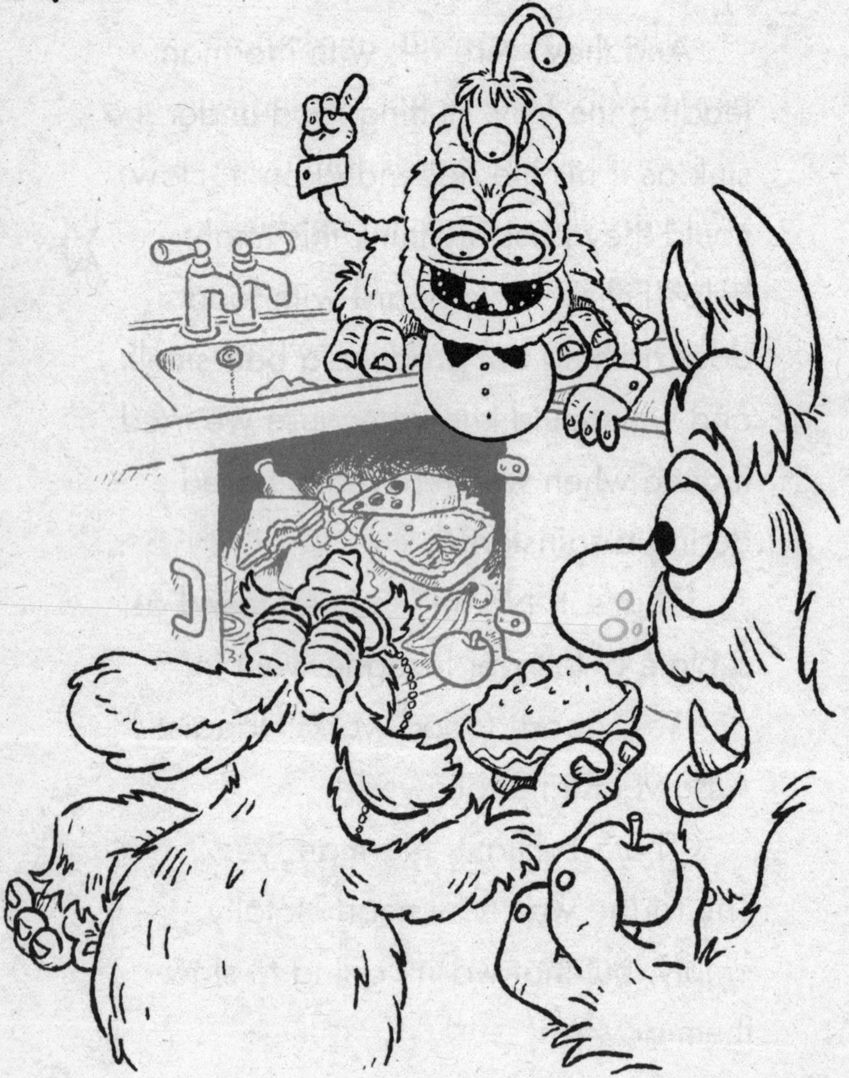

'The pipes are starving! More food! More food!' Fiend was rummaging through the cupboards, but there really was very little left to eat anywhere. It was all under the sink. Great. So even if the house didn't blow up, we would all starve. There was at least one more thing, though. Fiend had found my lunch box and was ripping off the lid. Well, I wasn't going to stop him, seeing as the contents looked completely yuck. Haggis was not quite so understanding, though.

'NO, NO, NO, NO, NOT MY PINE-OCCOLI-CAR -ANGE-ANANA!'

But in it went to join the rest of the ever-growing mound of gloop. It wasn't helping the plumbing situation, though; the noise was now really, really loud. It was complete insanity in my house and nobody was able to do anything about it, but that didn't stop Fiend having one last go at taking charge.

'This is your last chance, plumbing! Behave or else it's straight to bed!'

Haggis could also sense that all was decidedly not well. He came running over and cuddled me, something I don't mind admitting I was very grateful for at that precise moment in time.

'Oh, Eddie, Eddie, Eddie, I don't want to be a grown-up any more,' he wailed.

'EMERGENCY! EMERGENCY!'

cried Fiend, finally admitting to himself that his plans to save the day were simply not working just as Dad wandered in.

'Have you come to save us, mister dad human thingy person?' Haggis was actually starting to shake and I can't say I blamed him, especially if he thought Dad was the answer to our prayers.

'No, no, we've run out of crackers!' he shrieked, proving my point.

I let go of Haggis and ran across to Dad. I had one last plan of action. Maybe if I told the truth about how this had all begun then threw myself on his mercy, I might just be able to get him to snap out of it and rescue us all. Well, that was his job after all.

'Wait, Dad, please. This is all my fault. Because . . . because . . . OK, here goes. Because I wanted the

monsters to come upstairs, I flooded the basement. Now everyone's changed and the plumbing's trying to kill us.'

The faraway look in Dad's eyes vanished almost immediately and he became a grown-up again right in front of me.

'Mm, interesting.' Yup, it was there in the voice as well. My plan had worked. I had him back, as good as new. Now it was time to work on Mum. Luckily, she had just strolled in, also looking more mature than she had over the last few hours. It was all going well so far and the banging and crashing had stopped. Now I just had to . . . Hang on a minute. I was beginning to smell a rat and I don't mean like that

time Norman and Haggis decided to hide one in my school bag.

'Wait . . . how did you . . . and the noise?'

Mum smiled smugly at Dad, producing something from behind her back.

'You know, Eddie, if you're going to knock a hole in a pipe, it's best not to leave the screwdriver you did it with just lying around.' And with that, she displayed a short length of piping with the screwdriver jammed in for all the world to see. And there was no point in denying it was down to me because they clearly already knew exactly what had been

going on. But for how long had they
realized I had been up to no good? It
was all starting to make sense. They
must have found the pipe when they
went to the basement and decided to
carry on being naughty to teach me
a lesson.

'Wait a second . . . so you were just
pretending to be kids . . . and you made
all that noise like an explosion . . . just to
make me . . . You . . . you . . .

MONSTERS!'

Strong words, I know, but I was furious
with them. There I had been thinking
that they had lost the plot completely,
as well as worrying that the house was

going to boil over, and they had simply been planning the whole thing right from the word go.

Mum didn't even answer. They both just carried on grinning as Fiend stepped forward crossly.

'Easy, Ed. We're the only monsters around here. Remember?'

Don't Go Changing

I calmed down a bit eventually. Well, it was just so nice to have the house and my life back to normal. Parents were being parents and monsters were being monsters once again. It was almost beautiful enough to make me want to cry. While Mum had a go at fixing the plumbing by removing the big messy spider shape and replacing it with a few straight pieces, Fiend helped Haggis try to stuff Norman into a sleeping bag. As you can see, everything was just the way it was before.

'I never thought I'd say this, but it's

really good to have them back to their old selves again.' Dad was watching the monsters' antics and clearly agreed with me that all was right with the world once again.

'Fore!' shouted Haggis as he turned his attention to Fiend, using him as a golf ball and executing a perfect drive across the basement. Like I said, pure poetry in motion.

'Ahhh! I'm fine! I'm fine!' shouted Fiend,

leaping to his feet to show
that no bones or eyes
were broken like the last
time he had been used
this way by Haggis.

Mum stopped fiddling with the
pipework for a second and smiled
down on the scene of domestic monster
bliss playing out in front of her.
I wandered over.

'It's just like you always say: "A
place for everything and everything
in its place."' With that, I put my arm
round her. Well, it felt like a good time
to be the perfect little angel. Nobody
had really said anything about my
act of sabotage, but I certainly hadn't
forgotten about it. Maybe Mum had.

'Nice crawling, Eddie, but you're still in line for some serious punishment.' Who was I even kidding thinking it might have been a possibility?

Just then the pipes started rattling gently once again. Enough to make Haggis stop his game of 'Fiend golf' for a second to look worried. And even though I knew now that it was Mum who had been making all that noise, I was still a bit panicky myself. Well, you have to remember it had been loud enough to make me and the monsters think the house was going to explode, and that might have made us a teensy, weensy bit scared.

'I can't believe you made the pipes rattle like that from down here,' I said

as she tightened a screw here and turned a nut there. 'Still, don't you think it's time we got a professional in to fix the plumbing?'

'No need because I've decided to enrol you in three months of DIY evening classes.' Mum almost laughed as she said it. Wow, parents could be annoying as I'm sure you're only too aware.

'That's an imaginative punishment. I like it.' Dad was joining the 'Isn't Mum devious and shouldn't we all take our hats off to her for being so cunning?' club. His smug smile was soon wiped off, though.

'Good, because you're going, too.' It was Mum's turn to look pleased

with herself and Dad's to splutter indignantly.

'What? That's ridiculous. I . . .'

Mum cut him off short by pulling out a screw so that the pipes really began rattling hard once again. Dad looked nervous and immediately backed down.

'Evening classes, check,' he murmured as Angela wandered in and collapsed on the sofa. For some reason she really didn't look well.

'Nice time at the movies, Angela darling?' Mum was moving in for the kill. If you've ever seen a film about dinosaurs, you'll know the move I mean: when one of the meat-eating ones is getting ready to pounce on one of the plant-munching types.

'Ooh, ohh.' Even Norman could sense trouble when it was coming. Mind you, he'd been there when Fiend broke the news that Angela had gone to the cinema without proper permission of the grownup kind.

Angela lay down on the sofa, no doubt bracing herself for the mother of all telling offs. And I mean that literally.

'I can't believe you let me watch that . . . that thing.'

Nice play, sis. Looking terrified and upset in the hope that Mum would hold off on the punishment, thinking you had suffered enough. The girl was learning.

'So . . . the film was a bit scary then, was it? Not really suitable for someone of your age?' Mum was still sharpening her T.rex claws. This was going to be a quick kill.

'That monstrosity wasn't fit to be watched by anyone of any age. I'm going to be having nightmares for weeks now.'

'Or, in other words, mothers know best?'

Fiend moved across sympathetically. 'The lesson here is if you need a responsible grown-up, find someone who doesn't think this is funny. Hit it, Norm.'

And, needing no encouragement, Norman began making his famous armpit farting noises and, as one,

the monsters
collapsed
with laughter.
Angela seized
her moment,
grabbing the sleeping bag and cosying
down in it. Fiend stopped laughing for
a second to study her.

'Seriously, though, what's with the
sleeping arrangements? Your room's on
the first floor.'

'Not in a million years am I
going to be alone in the dark again.
And as you're the only things I know
that are more freaky-looking than
zombies, congrats: you're my new
bodyguards and I'm down here for
the night.'

Mum and Dad smiled
sweetly and turned to head back
upstairs. What was this? Were
they seriously going to let her
get away with it while I had to
suffer a punishment worse than
torture: going to DIY lessons with
my dad? I decided to get one last
moment of revenge in before we
left the monsters and Angela to it.

'You do know there's a large
spider down here about the size
of a poodle?' Well, it was only
fair to warn her about the pipe
monster, now safely removed by Mum,
but still sitting in a bucket in the corner
looking scary enough to the untrained
eye.

'Grow up, Eddie.' Angela clearly
didn't believe me so it seemed like
the right time to show her. I nodded
at Haggis and he wandered across to
fetch the bucket.

'Angela, meet Large Spider!'

'AAAAAGGGHHH!'

I suspect, though there's no way of finding out for certain of course, but I bet you could have heard her screams from Africa.

I guess, when it comes down to it, some things are meant to change, but others, like monsters and family . . . they're just fine the way they are.

Me & My MONSTERS™

for more monster mayhem
www.meandmymonsters.co.uk
or
www.meandmymonsters.com.au

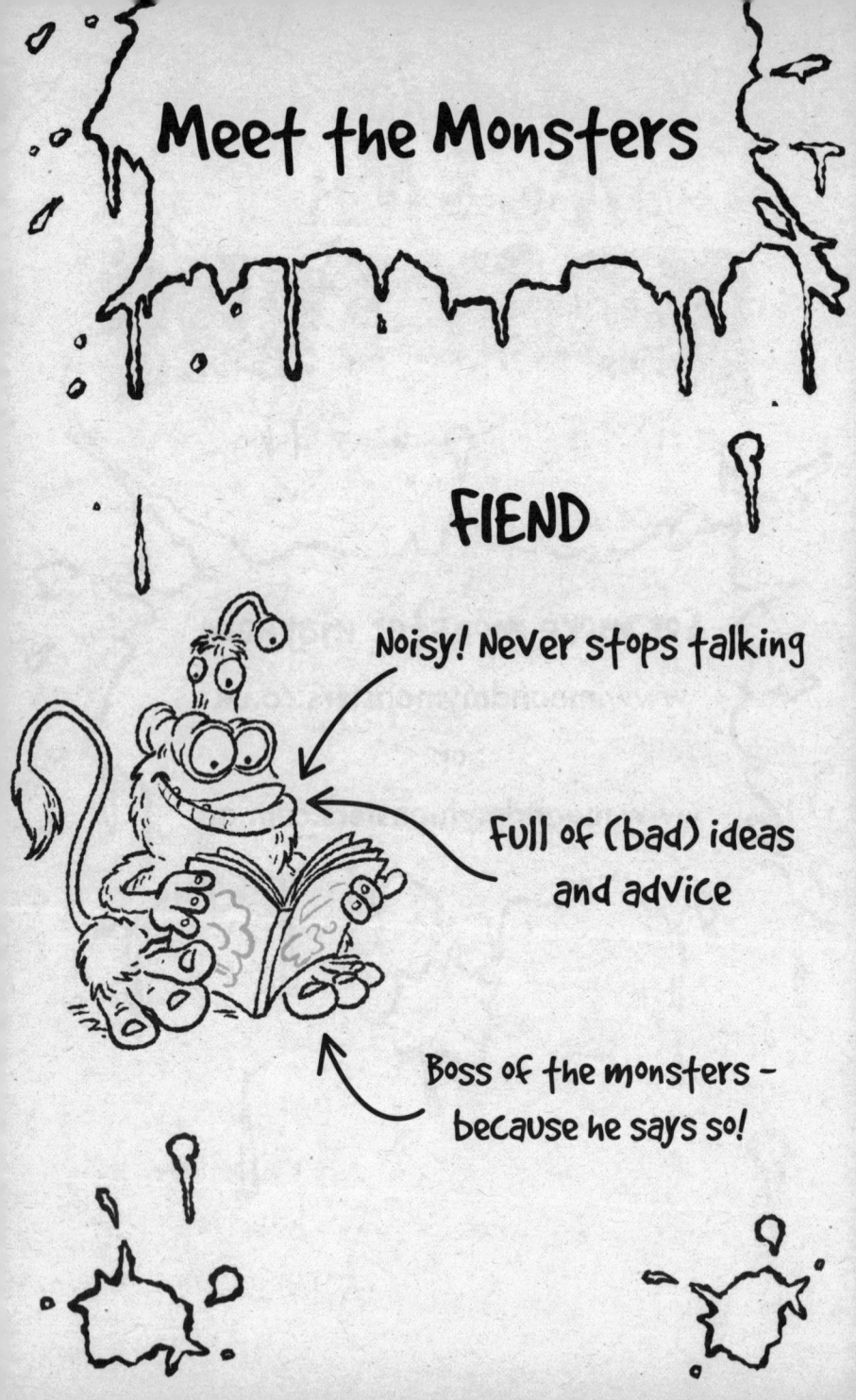

NORMAN

Big sticky-out nose

Makes weird noises – that's just how he speaks

He's not crazy he just seems that way.

HAGGIS

Whopping monster body

Scares very easily

Eats everything – you might just hear his belly ringing one day.

It all started with a Scarecrow.

Puffin is seventy years old.
Sounds ancient, doesn't it? But Puffin has never been
so lively. We're always on the lookout for the next big
idea, which is how it began all those years ago.

Penguin Books was a big idea from the mind of
a man called Allen Lane, who in 1935 invented
the quality paperback and changed the world.
**And from great Penguins, great Puffins grew,
changing the face of children's books forever.**

The first four Puffin Picture Books were hatched in 1940 and the
first Puffin story book featured a man with broomstick arms called
Worzel Gummidge. In 1967 Kaye Webb, Puffin Editor, started the
Puffin Club, promising to **'make children into readers'**.
She kept that promise and over 200,000 children became
devoted Puffineers through their quarterly instalments of
Puffin Post, which is now back for a new generation.

Many years from now, we hope you'll look back and
remember Puffin with a smile. **No matter what your age
or what you're into, there's a Puffin for everyone.**
The possibilities are endless, but one thing is for sure:
whether it's a picture book or a paperback, a sticker book
or a hardback, **if it's got that little Puffin
on it – it's bound to be good.**